THE MUSE

Amy Ellis

First Published 2022 by Amy Ellis, London UK

ISBN 978-1-7396986-0-7

A CIP catalog record for this book is available from the British Library.

The Muse is a work of fiction. Names, characters, businesses, places, events, locales, and incidents are either the products of the author's imagination or used in a fictitious manner. Any resemblance to actual persons, living or dead, or actual events is purely coincidental.

Cover Illustration by Jean Auguste Dominique Ingres (French, Montauban 1780–1867 Paris) and Workshop. Image from The Met.

Visit amy-ellis.com to learn more about the author's other books or sign up for her mailing list to be the first to hear about new works and other exclusive content.

THE MUSE

You know what happens to women like me?

There are a hundred and fifty thousand bodies
buried nearby in unmarked graves,

their headstones worn from long summers of rain, toppled
over and cut into flagstones, ground down by strangers'

footsteps on the threshold. There is no poets' corner for us:
the presence of our paint stained hands, the pigment powders

under our nails are blood moons, a dust storm
brought up from the Sahara. We turned the sky red.

I painted those covered up pictures layered in dust,
the portraits in your grandmother's attic are now unknown

retrospectives at the small gallery, my unread signature.
Someone paid me to paint those breasts in the rose garden and
  turn their lovers

into hidden pictures, discarded. Lewd pastel portraits
of your great-great-something grandmothers stripped

out of their corsets and chemise. They used to touch
each other too, pressed together like flowers

between the pages of your thrift store poetry books.
Invited me into their bedrooms and memorialised their bodies

where I am just bones somewhere, a skull, a sternum.
In memoriam of me and my breasts and the men

I let paint them and the lovers that held them.
I sold a hundred portraits of my body

to buy this nameless grave I'm in.

The Beginning

The day I learned to paint was the kind of crinkly, sugary
day that hurts to sink your teeth into.

My mother, at the table with her paints.
The blocks of colour dented with her dreams.

Her brush washed against the page
like a hand on a bruise

while my brush bled. She taught me
to mop up the mess.

The bristles feathered and flung colour
in all the wrong places. The purple bled

into green, a bruise shifting to the brown of riverbank.
We tapped the brushes against the side of glass until I
made

something in the shape of a petal and repeated until I
bloomed
a single flower that we set outside to dry in the sun.

Sunday Afternoons

are a ritual spent humming and licking
the brush to the page. The dented kitchen table turned

a stack of florals on the windowsill, piled up in my hope
chest among my unfinished linens.

I tried to wash away the future with watercolour while
my mother held the pictures to the light: it is an
   accomplishment

meant to be hung on the wall in the kitchen between
church and supper and putting the children to bed

to impress a man. A pastime
not a lifetime of watercolour.

My Father

My father was a wig maker,
spent his days hunched over a bust
sewing the long hairs into place.

His spectacles sliding down his nose
as the early winter sun waned in the sky.
He could afford a whole house just for us,
and was thankful for a small family.

While the other homes teemed
with small children, crying
in their sodden nappies,
ours was a sanctuary of four.

Love

And in those long afternoons
around the kitchen table
my mother would tell me

stories of how she met our father
and their long engagement
where he would write her long poems

and she would illustrate them, saving
the pages as a story for her children.

In church I gaze over my shoulder
and crave the contact of a man
I could marry and carry on the habit

of swirling paint in a glass jar, leaving
rings behind on the table full of blues
and the muddled purple of too much colour.

I'd paint every flower he'd bring me
and save them until their edges curl
and the pages crumble away like ash

or dust or bodies in the grave,
forgotten in that dull floral of decay.

The Shop

The childhood afternoons watching my father
in his shop, sewing each strand into place,
curling, moulding, fixing a hairstyle worthy
of a wealthy customer.

Out from under my mother's feet
my toes tapped the floorboards
as the hours passed, helping little
but providing good company in the quiet shop.

On days his customers would come in,
I stood by the door, offered them tea
and stayed silent, obedient, mostly invisible
but for the few who noticed me standing there, often
smiling in vague acknowledgement before turning away.

But the man with the emerald eyes would bring me
  trinkets:
buttons and ribbons, a shiny red apple,
a single paintbrush finer than any I'd ever used.

Married Off

My sister, Betty, married a baker,
A suitable match and she lived close,
unburdened and baking.

We'd sit in the windows
of their shop on the quiet days
and split sticky buns,
lick our fingers and laugh

but when I left her she was rolling
the dough and kneading early in the morning,
his fingers in her hair, sugar
and flour rising as the ovens heat

and burn and smoulder. The steam
on the windows. She doesn't mention it
when I visit her, writes her new initials in the panes
and erases them with the palm of her hand.

Women's Work

At the table it's women's work:
shelling beans, making bread, nursing
babies, soothing scrapes, arranging daisies.

Picking meats and fruits in the market to feed us,
filling baskets, settling tabs, bartering and bargaining.

Impressive and skilled, these watercolours
painted up to win over a man, to marry him, to learn

that the bedroom is women's work:
our bodies growing and bleeding and working
to make him a son.

The Muse

I stopped looking for a husband the day I met her—
smudged fingers spotting her face as she sat sketching

in the gallery. I watched her studying the broken figure
of an ancient man. She was rebuilding him.
His fractured bones repaired on her page.

They don't let us attend the life
drawing classes, she said,
so these are the bodies I know.

I returned to that room often to find her missing.
In the hollow belly of a whale, I'd watch the unmoving
marble of the man until I knew his every bone and sinew,
until

I was ready to try to build him in my own hand—my first
body,
shared with her. A broken God, raging.

The Empty Palette

The quiet hollow of an empty home:
only me, sipping tea among the breakfast dishes

while my mother paces the market—a basket of eggs
and bread and varying shades of wilted greenery.

Paintbrushes ticking against glass. A rose. A poppy.
Chrysanthemums. A whole vase of torn scraps of paper,

little petals of water to keep the brushes wet.
Pack them away carefully, tucked

beneath a pile of linens, every day, little petals,
little practises, little spells to birth new

watery blossoms, pale and awash
with the last of my colour.

Meeting

I visited often and sketched the same body she drew in the
museum:
a man born of marble and chisel: hands, body, face—
my charcoal scraps, the torn edges of my page.

A man sat down beside me and sketched the same statue
with hands that understood the strength and sinew
the bone and joint and brokenness.

When he finished, he left the drawing for me
and walked away—I didn't even ask for his name.
In the stunned museum silence

the statues jutted like jagged teeth
from the floor. The gallery opened its mouth
and swallowed me whole.

The Wide Views of Elsewhere

The first time I walked into a gallery, I shook the
   afternoon off like a raincoat,
little droplets of chores and future husbands scattered
   along the walkway like petals.

Art became more than ditsy watercolours in the kitchen.
   It was suddenly the seascapes: the raging
infinity of ocean tossing a boat full of men into pieces.
   The pastorals, a herd of cows grazing

through the long lazy afternoons chewing cud in the sun,
   fawns kneeling at the altar
of field and meadow eternally. The wide views of
   elsewhere.

The intimacy of a woman sat still for her painter, the vast
   white snowdrifts of her chest heaving
for hours. The long conversations they'd had as he turned
   her face toward the light

his hands manipulating her into this apparition, a ghost, a
   second coming
of woman. I can see the yellows he used, the sunlight, the
   long rays

coming in through the window. It was more than the
   flowers from the markets
bowing their heads in fragile age as I painted their petals'
   wrinkled silk shattering.

When I Saw Him Next

We drew, listening to the hush
of our charcoal etching
out secrets like whispers

the pauses of cautious anticipation
the forbidden knowledge
that we were there, alone

together. *These are the bodies*
I know, I said to him.
I brought him my vases

of watercolours and when he found me
next, he left a fresh box of watercolours
beside me, touched a gray-marked

hand to my pink cheek—brighter.

Sculpt

We had been there so many days
swallowed up by a mouth full
of marble jutting up, ground down
and chiselled away into bodies of men.

We knew them, their unmoving
forms frozen for centuries
just to pose for us.

When no one was looking
sometimes I'd reach out to
touch them, cradle the cold curve
of a cheek in my hand, fold

my fingers into their
hardened hands, brittle
and rigid in mine.

He tells me what it's like
to paint a person and know
the lines of the living:

how they move, how they change
the softness and the hardness of them
the impossibility of perfection.

He takes my hands and folds
his fingers into mine. I can feel
his heartbeat in the palm of my hand.

The Bouquet

And soon I am painting faces in the flowers
and as the buds unfold there are bodies

limber in their centres, legs and arms crawling
like insects across the long silk sheets, delicate

petals and brittle limb, I let each bloom reveal
its character like a flock of ballerinas slowly

skittering across a stage like birds
heading home from a long winter.

Stitching

I have always laced up my backbone
and stitched the whole bible into into my samplers
taught to me with the long complacency of childhood
and inescapable prison of age and sex and gender and
suddenly

I was surrounded by a shrinking sea, wading out
to the long sandbar sketched up by a scrawling hand.
Violets on Sunday afternoons, laughing, gossiping.

A brush stroke. A plate of biscuits dusted with sugar
like crystals catching the light, crumbling away
like sand whipped up in the wind, falling

through the hourglass. Afternoons and afternoons
and tomorrows until there won't be anymore and I am
married, teaching samplers and sunflowers to my
daughters too.

When We Had Exhausted Their Bodies

When our hands could sketch
them from muscle memory alone,
that was when he took my hand
for the first time and offered
a space for me in his studio.

His hand cupped the round of my
cheek, listening for the echoing
footsteps of approach, the hollow
chalky sound of shoes meeting marble.

I'll show you how to draw real life.
For the moment it was just us
in the city, touching each other
in the mouth of a museum, swallowed
up by the statues. *I can make a real*
painter out of you.

I could not pull my lips apart
and when I left it was raining
and the streets smelled hot with steam,
the summer slipping away like a lover
returning to her chamber in the dark.

The House

I hadn't eaten the first morning I visited him
and everything felt opaque as I walked through the wet

streets, a morning fog, an empty mind, empty
body in the heave and surge of a city.

He pulled me in, guided me through the dark
hallways and stairways of the house to a studio so full of
  light—

He opened a chest to show me the breadth of his colours.
I painted the light of the room and his hand

guided me—mixing my first colours in oil and smoothing
the thick pigments across the freshly stretched skin
of canvas. He wiped the paint from my hands at the end.

A First Canvas

A studio
that overlooked
the river. A trip
to the market.
A canvas cured
and hung on the wall
of his studio,
shining under the light
of a setting sun.
It felt like
a promise
made of glass.

Patience

Betty did not have the patience to paint, spun
circles around the kitchen table and my hands
would rush to keep up with her

arms spinning like sugar in the air, whipped up
to featherweight, flying. I learned to follow her
motion, catch her mid-leap, mid-

song, arms up—a kitchen ballet.
I painted the way her skirts lifted
in the wake of her, the way the air

whipped at the pages and curled the ends.
A study in motion, swirling absentmindedly in childhood
splendour, pastel Sunday afternoons

a whole church full of ribbons in my sketchbook,
a company of dancers stood at the wings waiting to fly.

Morning

In the mornings I tried to lay in bed and listen to the sounds of waking:
my mother starting the fire, warming the bread, the steam rising from her tea.

It was a luxury, time spent alone with no reward,
my sister was visiting, chattering about her violet dreams.

I tried to remember mine but only see the vague
shapes of colours: cerulean and chartreuse

behind my eyes. I should be there, adding more logs to the fire,
peeling potatoes, cracking eggs, washing the crumbs from their plates

but I'm here, tucked away, stealing myself from them, waiting
in the blue glow of early day, painting scenes on the ceiling.

Brush strokes and pencil sketches tucked away for later:
an afternoon with his hands teaching me how to hold mine.

Routine Secrets

In the nectarine glow of afternoon,
he poured a glass of wine and lounged

behind me as I tried to paint the ships on the water
their sails opening and folding down

like lilies opening for the morning
and sealing shut for the shimmer of night,

folding around their masts, men clung
to their ropes, pulling

as the sun burned golden
and cast a shadow across his face

as he watched me, like a God,
trying to make the light.

Let Me Draw You

Wait. Let me draw you like that,
and my face felt like a flame, reddening
to the ruby of pomegranate pulled apart,
the juice bleeding into my skin.

I was still, a sculpture for him to sketch,
and I watched his eyes flit from the page to my face,
my body. I felt a twitch in my fingers that matched
the rhythm of the charcoal traveling in arches,
in wild but careful lines.

An Excuse Quickly Becomes a Lie

A market becomes a gallery.
An afternoon mass is the portrait of a body
posed and twisted into distorted shapes.

His maid, Rebecca, would purchase extra for me and I
would leave my body there in exchange for her
wilting herbs, a basket of flowers, yesterday's eggs.

Come home, empty a basket onto the table.
They were out of carrots, I'd say. *All they had were sunflowers.*

The Colours of My Desires

It became a game of give and take
and he would give me the freedom
and skills to paint a masterpiece,
mix up the colours of my desires
through orange autumnal afternoons.

But some days, he would ask me to stop
and I would sit for him as he
studied me, sketched me, surrendered me
to canvas, and after long my face

would surround the walls of his studio
in colour and black and white, a mural
of me invoking the muses as we washed
the days with cerulean blues.

The Coffee House

On a slow afternoon, when the clouds
and the light were low, we took a carriage
to the coffee house he frequented: a dark room,
cozy with firelight, bustling

with the arguments and
articulations of men.
The theories and politics of art.

Men's art. Women's art.
The differences between.
And I, the lone woman,

sat quietly, sipping a steaming mug
of bitter coffee with John's hand
slipped around me, gripping my waist

like a ventriloquist, urging
my lips to speak but there,
in that room, they could not.

Rebecca

She would punctuate the days
with a rattling tray of tea
or biscuits or little bowls of fruit.

She would serve us and linger
to see the progress we'd made
on a portrait, another moody

still life, candlelit oysters
and lemon peel curls.

It was a quiet, contemplated lingering,
hanging out by the door, clinging
to the empty tray, watching

as he laughed and touched
the side of my cheek with his
paint stained fingers, a whole

rainbow hidden under his nails,
smeared across his smock.
When we finished she would retreat

with the tottering cups and bowls, the plates
of crumbs and disappear down the narrow stairs
to the kitchen to wash and scrub and fill

a basket by the door for me with her
unwanted acquisitions from the market:
carrots, a single potato, a handful of wilted herbs.

A silent saviour buying my alibi with tea
and bruised apples, watching us paint, tracing
the brush strokes with her eyes then

closing the door behind her
as her skirts whispered through the halls.
Somewhere down the long stairs and corridors

the kettle whistled and she removed it
from the stove, pouring herself a cup
to drink alone, imagining.

Some Afternoons

I would stop to see Betty
on the way home from the studio

my arms full of desires
and parsley and artichokes

and she would tell me I still had
the tell-tale smudge of teal on my cheek.

Bones

When he asked me to his house I knew
what he wanted and I was expecting it some day.

When he asked me to take off my clothes
I felt it deep in me: the long dread

as he looked at me and remarked *look at the light*
on your bones and gestured toward my hands,

the bones pulled up in arches, claws gripping,
like spiders sitting and waiting for their prey.

He took me

for my first glass of wine
that evening in a steamed up tavern
full of voices and closeness.

The sputtering fire. The warmth
of the glass in my hand.
He touched

my face again.
I leaned into him aching
for that perfect

scratch—to touch
the deep aching itch
I feel burning

somewhere between
corset and petticoat and
body.

We stayed there
a long time
until the world

spun faster beneath
us and he took me
home and left me
at the door—

After the wine

I thought I knew aching until I ached
after him, or because of him:

the wine he poured me went straight
to my head and my stomach pitched:

a ship tossed in the sea, a hand scooping
the seeds from a gourd, broken open.

I stayed in bed to recover from him
and my mother mopped the sweat from my brow

with her hands, misunderstanding
my ailments, made me tea and toast

to settle my stomach, a raging sea inside me,
heaving upwards, pitching and listing

while I wondered—was he sweating in his bed?
Did his tongue feel as heavy as mine—a sunken ship—

and when she left me to suffer alone, I curled
up inside myself and imagined his heavy tongue

tasting me. I licked my fingers to taste
the salt from my skin and I liked it.

Posing

The next session, I posed for him
and we made it ordinary

to remove layers of clothes
and distort my body, take it

into new positions:
stretching, arching,

the throb of holding,
of being looked at

I barely breathed,
flushed cheeks, the sheen

of sweat translated to
effervescent glow in his work

my skin finally breathing,
my whole body so free—

a courtesan slung
over her unmade bed

Venus revealing her breasts
on the walls of a gallery—a surprise

a simmering something
bubbling to my surface

so untouched and unknowing.
It didn't feel as shameful

as it should have been,
my body slung lazily in the sun.

Small Mirrors

Sometimes I fragment:
stare at myself in pieces

in the small mirror
in my room, sketch

myself into minutia
each detail smaller

and smaller, straight down
to the cells, the little buds

that build me. A scar. A vein.
The creases in my skin. My hands.

My eye. My ears. Hip bone.
My left toes. The folds

between my legs
aching.

we licked the sugar from our hands.
Don't let him touch you—she said.

I thrust my fingers into the hollow shell
of pastry, sugar glazed and hardened off.

But what does it mean
when I let him look?

Canvas

On the long afternoons when he'd paint
me, I studied him too

with my hands posed how he told me to hold them,
I would watch his eyes work

through every inch of me in a studious gaze
with the curiosity and seriousness

of a student who is entirely absorbed in his work
and yet utterly lost. But, oh,

how his hands moved the brush,
slopping through the heaps of paint,

pressed to canvas and back again.
The air held still—

thick with dust and sun as the afternoons
waned and at the end

I stretched my limbs and dressed in the tall studio
   windows
watching the tall ships draw their sails and groan

down the river. He would touch
the curl of my shoulder

before I could pull all the fabric back into place
and we would stand there bathing
in the intimacy of our secret.

Mutual

He let me flip through the sketchbooks to study
the way he drew other women, their bodies,

big bowls of fruit spilling over, their hands,
the curves of their stomachs, their roundness
their jagged edges, breast and body.

Who else he had draped over this chaise
her clothes crumpled on the floor, her unlaced corset—
Hold still, he said, tracing my lines as I

shivered.

Home

My mother shelled peas at the kitchen table
her knuckles bending and pulling at each shell letting
each piece fall gently into the wooden bowl before her.

I sat down and scraped the last bit of blue
from my thumb before reaching out
for a pod to peel. I admired how green—

dreamt up the colours I'd need to create such a small
part of a bowl, the deeper emeralds in the shadows
out-shined by the sea greens, the brights in the highlights.

I stole a few and placed them in my mouth like a sweet.
Where have you been? Empty handed again, I tore at the edge
of a pod that refused to open and ripped the seeds from the
shell,
feeling the heat from the fire burn my neck.

Lore

In art you can be many things
and in many places all at once.

There are those who paint themselves
into the portraits of past and stories

until they become the lore. I am not
much more than the portrait on his easel:

half finished and blank spaces.
The patchwork of colour, layered up

beginning.

When She Found Us

It was a washout, the whole city was a wall of water
flushing the shit and smells from the streets.

I was standing on the threshold of his home, huddled
in his arms as we sheltered from the sheets

of rain. That is the moment it fell apart: the stones,
the glass houses. My mother walking by and knowing

me in the arms of a man she didn't know.
My hands were the rainbow of deceit. That afternoon

I'd painted with the murky colours of a storm, mixed up
the afternoon like a crystal ball, a future-gazing fortune-teller.

And from her tight-lipped reticence I knew what would
happen if I didn't
pull away from him and leave him on the wet steps.

I followed her silence though the streets while the rain
decided to cease and the clearing skies lightened up

to mock us. We imprisoned ourselves in the wordless house
where the fire was smoking with damp wood, a shroud fallen
over us,

wondering what was next for the ruined girl with an
unfinished hope
chest. She found the courage to tell my father while I
remained

locked away beneath the covers, smelling the oils
on my skin and when they found me there, I could not see

through the tears of my future, peeling away like paint
from my hands in little pearls. They were the only things I could

eventually wash clean.

Wreckless

My mother was afraid to handle knives that night,
her temper boiling over as she stirred the pot
on the stove, simmering and steaming

while I sliced bread, chewed over the carelessness
of my afternoon, reckless woman wrecking her future
like a hammer to the hand, splintering bone and blood.

We spooned the food from our bowls at dinner and let it fall,
appetite-less, feeling the churn of regret in the bottom
of my stomach. I could not listen to the quiet

of my parents' shame as my father cleared the shock
from his throat. I left the table before he could pluck
the words from behind the obfuscating anger clouding the room.

I fled the house and wound the long streets,
stumbling over the cobblestones to the threshold
of my reputation where I found him waiting

there with the same paint on his face, holding
the empty space I'd been plucked from so I could slot
right back into place, a missing piece to a broken vase—

kintsugi—back together. *Come inside.*
Come inside with me.
And I did.

The Last Portraits

I want to paint
I said and we
ascended

the stairs
to the studio
where he lit

the lamps and
we painted
hurried portraits

of each other
by candlelight,
humming and

whispering *no,*
that's not quite
right while

the sun sank
finally
in a darkness

that hung blue,
the orange candles
sputtering flames

poking holes
into the dark
corners of the room

but it was too
dark to see
the true colours.

We retreated,
the final
moments

of colour,
a faded murky
pool plunged

into black
thick as blood
as he held me.

The Goodbye

When we finished
our final paintings
he took me

to the bar down
the street, our hands
still coated in a rainbow

of oils. He slapped
the table. He ordered
another glass of wine.

I was trying
to tell him
goodbye.

If you leave,
you will never paint
again.

He reached
for me. He held
my hand. I felt

for the places
where his paintbrush
rested when he showed me

how to make the light.
All the hours, the colours
are wasted on you.

I drank a glass of wine
too many until the world swirled—
a canvas shimmering

with fresh paint.
There was music echoing
in the city. We danced

in the street. He held
my hand. He kissed
my neck. I knew

I was never going home
I would collect
my belongings in the morning.

First Night

I let him unlace
me, thread
the ribbons
through the rivets
and pull.

It was cotton
against skin
and the feeling
of his hands
on me

I could feel
the wear
of him: golden
hour, an orange
room set fire
and I let him

trace the highlights
and shadows
of my figure.
He knew my curves
better than me.

He could close
his eyes and find
where my neck
curled into shoulder
where my body
folded into itself:

an envelope,
a letter, ready
to be slit
open and read
like a memorised
poem, sung.

Thin Petals

I'd never seen a naked man
in the flesh before that night.

I thought I'd know what I'd see.
I'd studied the naked sculptures of men

for months, drawn and shaded their
most intimate parts, but to touch

the warm skin. I knew it was a secret
that could not be returned: a guarded

knowledge, carefully concealed and then
opened like a long awaited bloom

at the end of a long winter, so pink
and warm against me. The next morning

he awakened to the sound of my brush
chiming against glass as I painted

the delicate petals opening up, the thin
watercolour leaves of me, practically
transparent in this new light.

The Return

I went back in the dark to find the candles smoking
and the air dense with the smell of burning.

I thrust open the door and walked into a room
that was simultaneously the past and present:

yesterday and today. Arms around me, my mother clung
to my hair and body. I smelled like wine and sweat and skin.

My head throbbed as she began to understand what I'd done:
my ruin, the dissolution of monasteries, the reclamation of
 the stones.

A willing participant in my own shattered future. Fists
on the table. My mother behind the bedroom door.

The tightly sealed house felt draughty. A candle extinguished
and the smoke curled into a question.

I wished this was a painting: all orange and blue and haze. I
 bit
into an apple from the bowl and chewed its mealy flesh
 between my teeth

while my father retrieved my sketchbook and ripped the
 pages from its spine.
They glowed and smoked in the hearth like wet leaves,
 smothering.

I returned to his house empty handed and burrowed
myself in his body, breathed in the smell

of his pipe smoke, shushed by the sound of his heart
pounding like a wave breaking the coast into sand.

Rebecca drew me a bath

and sat beside me as I lowered my body
into the steaming tub until every inch of my skin

engulfed in warmth. Water slithering around me,
floral and murky with my own film of sin.

She watched me while the water cooled
with vacant eyes that followed the steam

as it curled away from me, my body pink
with heat and shame as I'm watched by a stranger.

It's a strange feeling to be watched
rather than looked at: observed.

Pomegranate Seeds

He showed me new things: painted
then fed me the seeds of a pomegranate

with his fingers, pushing them into my mouth
until they burst and I crunched their flesh,

like bones, between my teeth.
The curl of lemon peel. The bite

of grapefruit. He slid oysters down
my throat and cracked the claws

of lobsters, dipped their sweet flesh
in butter and devoured. He served me,

poured me a chalice of wine and licked
the blood from my lips.

Creation

On nights I needed to be alone
I slept in a room beside the studio
where I could smell the paints curing
on their canvases, worked into their final
forms as the day glowed from morning blue
to golden afternoon. Red sunrise. The purple
of midnight. I mixed the colours in my mind
just the way he showed me, our hands
were prisms, creating colour from light.
Grinding, stirring until we were satisfied
and the broken bristles of our brushes
found the right way to stroke.

I'd been wearing the same dress for days

When my mother appeared in the doorway of the house
we'd hidden away in, our bodies naked and covered
in a rainbow of paint splatters that freckled our faces.

Rebecca poured us tea in the parlour where the fire
raged in the hearth, a sputtering song to pierce the silences
with cracks and pops, a series of sparks.

We sat before a trunk of my belongings, my whole life
packed up and delivered with stony silence, the chipping
of china cup against saucer between empty sips.

It wasn't a peace offering but a parting gift. *I'm sorry*
I gave you this, she said, mopping a splatter
of vermilion from my cheek with her thumb.

I don't believe

in the ruined woman—
a vessel broken open
can be repaired
a toppled abbey
becomes a garden.

Breakfast Song

In the morning
he pours me tea
and tucks my loose
hair behind my ears.

He paints me a morning
portrait. He mixes the muted
tones of early light
and relearns my curves.

He creates the dark spaces
in me. Sees me
for the way I am:
the way my body folds
and falls and lies
in the unmade bed.

When I Left

I didn't think it would be so different forever.
The unintended consequences of ruin are a bathtub
warmed by the hands of someone else's labour.

It is a meal served up and eaten in fashionable
politeness, candelabra, silver fork. The nose bubbles
of champagne. The long afternoons spent scraping
the paint from my board with a brush and letting it dance.

I have been born anew out of the silence of the past—
the unanswered letters, the people you leave behind
become graveside monuments, the broken bones
of a wounded corpse still twitching in the grave.

I tried not to think of it too much but between the pigment,
when the colours blur to the sooty darkness of hearthstone
and kitchen table, I can smell the lilacs we used to paint
or is it simply Rebecca returning with her arms full of bloom.

Visiting Betty

Sometimes her husband walks in, his face dusted with flour
and his cheeks rosy from the hot ovens as he looks in and watches.

He smells like dough, rising and bubbling. He leans over and kisses
the top of her head. He asks what I painted that afternoon, the colours

of sunflowers still smudged into my hands. The answer's a whole vase
filled with bloom. I watched a ladybird crawl across the petals, the tickle

of its step shaking the pollen from the centre: the whole table covered in gold dust.
I don't tell him this, their eyes watching me were so green,

flashing looks of cautionary tale at me, his worried
shuffle back to the roaring ovens like a hush.

How to Listen, Obey, and Lay the Brush Down

In the violet afternoons of Sundays, I had painted
the views of my future: the sunflowers hanging
over my bed, their heavy heads watching the faces
of my children sleep and whispering to me
all the things I could've had if I'd known
how to listen, obey, and lay the brush down.

There is a drawer in our house with my paintings in it,
that I can open and look at the splashes of colour,
the quick sketch between feedings and keeping the kitchen
clean.
There is no woman drawing sculptures in the gallery.
There is no man asking me to take my clothes off.

There is no studio, no sunlight, no strangers undressing.
In the midnight quiet, my husband sleeps. There is a
child
suckling on my breast. There is a candle extinguished
on the table, its smoke curling into an unknown timeline
of linens and children and the long expanse of time
where
I do not paint. At the end, I admire the flowers in the
vase,
dried up as I finish, their petals dropped.

Still Life

I painted a vase that reminded me of me—
there were flowers falling from their stems
but I painted them like they were new
and smashed the vase at the end.
This picture will hang somewhere beside
a violin, a tapestry, a portrait of a female nude
and no one will know how beautiful
I became when he ruined me.
This is his bedroom. This is his mouth
on me. I can open these tulips
with my tongue and suck all the nectar out.

First show

He entered my still life into the exhibition
and there it hung—a bouquet opened up

petals splintering and spreading, hands, legs
opening night, I wrote to my mother, my father

to invite them then stood watch beside my name
posted on the wall for everyone to see

me, opening up, a night blossom that unfurls
slowly and fades away by morning.

They don't come to see me
standing there—blooming.

Beautiful Work

Instead, a man I vaguely recognised stood beside me
and I counted my breaths until he leaned in close
to say *beautiful work—I'd buy it if it wasn't spoken for.*

It was the depth of early morning darkness
before I remembered him standing in my father's shop
offering me a spare ribbon pulled from his pocket
or, one time, the first lemon I'd ever seen,

so bright and round. I bit right into its bitter flesh
and felt my mouth dry pucker and dry out
just as it had when he leaned in that evening.

The Portrait

As I mixed the colours until they matched his own, he painted
the background of a portrait: a long velvet curtain

and golden tassels to tie it back to reveal
nothing or everything. The spectre of white

canvas where a man would stand,
glowing centrefold. I am not a portrait artist.

But you are, he said. Those hours spent sketching
broken hands held indefinitely stretching endlessly

into the centuries only for me to come along and draw
them trapped there, my unwilling models.

He told me to mix the colours of skin and see
what kind of rainbow the flesh was really made of.

I sketched the face of a man I did not know
for a sum I could not fathom. I helped him
shade the jawline. I put the line between his lips.

The Fallout

While there were whispers, the was little fallout.
I woke up, I painted with him, I covered my hands in blue

and pressed them to his skin. I disappeared from a few
of the closely intertwined social circles, dropping the links

and separating like a magic trick, a parlour game,
like coins into a fountain, so lucky.

I watched the ships sail by. I layered the paint into gardens
on my canvas. A bouquet somewhere between blooming

and falling apart. I didn't receive another letter from my
mother.
I assumed she knew I was well.

Charlotte

She poured me a cup of tea and inspected the lines
and symmetry of me, the canvas weave, the texture of my
skin.

She bought the bouquet at the exhibition, stood beside me
and saw right away through the way my irises curled.

The rules suddenly didn't matter anymore, a new future
unfolding, a fan feathering and fawning like a whisper.

When I returned home, we celebrated into the night,
uncorking
bottles and curling into each other, bodies blooming.

He painted me

while I touched myself, exploring my own
insides, trying to understand how my body

works and winds up and screams out on the hour.
I thought of the statue I'd drawn, the trays of oysters,

the strength it takes to split a peach with your bare
fingertips, to pull the flesh from the stone.

He drew his fingers in my mouth, the trapezoidal
fragments of light from the sinking sun, the horizontal

afternoons spent orange in wonder. I understood
the melody of my body, the texture of the moon.

We created a routine—

ate breakfast in quiet company
while he read the morning paper,

blotting his inky fingers on the hem of the linens,
drank the dregs of his lukewarm tea.

We painted until luncheon, a cold
plate of cheese and meat and bread.

He had a glass of sherry in the late afternoon
and undressed me before dinner to
kiss the landscape of my inner thighs.

We ate our dinner off the silver,
clinked our glasses of wine
in the sputtering glow of candlelight.

Sold

He sold a painting of me, my whole body
in shades of pinks and creams, the inside

of a nectarine, the bloom of red when you bite
right into the centre, scrape your teeth
against the rough surface of the stone.

He sold me to a patron who hung me, alone,
in a private room where he could touch himself

in the company of his cigar smoke, view
the whole of me, her unmoving lips unable

to open and talk back, lick the tip of her brush
and polish out the imperfections.

Tracing Paper

That night I stood in front of the mirror
and sketched the outline of my body

knowing it's still hanging elsewhere—
a body so disconnected from mine

but still mine though the colours were mixed
and stroked smoothly by someone else's hand

knowing just where I curve and split and come
back together again. His hands on me in the bedsheets

our bodies wrinkling like sketchbooks, licking
the paint from our hands. I curl a piece of charcoal

over page and make a new nude, hard
line and broken tip—would someone buy me
if I looked like this?

Unsold

Some days he piled
into a carriage with all
of his pieces of me
and returned with
his arms just as full
as the moment he left.

Those nights
spent smelling the drink
from the quiet
cocoon of my bed,
waiting

for the shattering
the bleeding
the clean up
the morning

with Rebecca serving me
eggs and bread
alone and I grind
the pigments
in the daylight

while he moans
in his bed.
I paint the sick green
of his face, the arch
of his spine as he purges.

A Dream

I am in my own kitchen in shades of blue
and white shiny tiles and copper pans steaming
with smells and soups and screams.

I am kissed by a tall man with no face.
He puts on a hat and leaves
into the fog outside the door—

a sulphurous cloud hanging
yellow and murky outside my door
where I wait for him to return

after a long day of being faceless
in the real world. While he is gone
I search for my paints in my house

and find nothing but a pile
of monogrammed linens
with someone else's name on them.

But When He Sells Me, How He Celebrates Me

The coins chiming in his pocket
like a lark breaking dawn.

And somewhere, while I share
a bottle of wine and a bed with this man

another sees me silently hanging
in his study where I am not

fleshy and bloody and bony and
would never paint another man

with his legs spread, twisted up
inside me. She would never do that.

A Patron

I visited Charlotte and sat in a smoky room, the fireplace
was chucking
out soot that clung to your clothes and skin and stung
your eyes red.

The gilded frames draped in cobwebs and wallpaper
flocked but faded.
We ate sweets her servants brought in on plates as brittle
as bones,

their pink painted flowers hidden beneath a cake, a tart.
Her hands folded
in her lap, her silver hair plated and tucked neatly in a
nest on top of her head.

She would tell me the names of other women who'd
painted for her before, the bodies
of their models draped along the walls of hallway and
staircase and bedroom.

Other women, skirting by or simply hobbyists, but no one
painting
themselves in the way that I can: a body, a bouquet, a
bone dry tongue

in my mouth.

Afternoons with Rebecca

I liked to sit with her
as she polished the silver
or mended the holes
in his paint-stained clothing,
her needles tracing the rips
and tears like a railroad, zipping
up and down through the city,
the countryside, the jagged
and broken coasts.

I practised on her never-still hands
drawing out the roughness
of her fingers as she carefully
stitched or polished or peeled
the skin off potatoes for dinner,
smoothed the sheets on our bed,
swept the cobwebs from the corners
and the dust from our still lifes.

She had a soft alto hum that bubbled
up between the silence we
sometimes settled into between
needle and thread and the clatter
of silver sliding back into the drawer.

Breathing

I learned to paint figures from the steady unmoving
sculptures of men, carved up into blocks of marble

and weather worn, broken bits chipped off and left
behind,
nameless disembodied pieces of men. I sketched them
broken

and tried to put them back together again with imaginary
fingers and mouths, reconstructed noses. When a live
woman

entered the studio, she arrived whole and in colour, pink
and breathing. She wasn't solid and stone, flexed her
ankles

in the pose, changed her gaze and watched us as we
made her new. The sun curled around her as the time
shifted

from late morning through afternoon, casting longer
shadows on her face that spread down. I had to change

and move with her, make her seem still yet living,
colour her right, peachy morning melting to a rosy
afternoon,

she would reach for a drink just as I thought I knew her
and the whole mood would shift. Quickly, get her

just like that, the little smirk, distilled down to her real self
—

whoever that is—her real self as I saw her.

She's quiet and reveals nothing but new shades
as the day goes and at dusk she admires our work

while she dresses, her fingers full of her modelling wages.
She says nothing, just traces her finger along her chin

as she studies mine, checking to see if it feels quite right.
It probably doesn't, our own views are the same but the
visions

are utterly different. His looks better
than mine and took half the time.

Sketch

Even though beards were in fashion, he kept his face clean
shaven.
He said his former beard was caked in paint from the
quiet contemplation

of fingers reaching up absently as he watched the light
land on the landscape of a body, a lake, a riverbed.

When he dozed in the studio late morning
sun glinted and I painted him a rainbow

of watercolours swirling around his naked
face and hung it on the studio walls

surrounded by the arched backs of women,
the pale pinks of skin framed him.

Another Dream

I am home the day
my brother died
his little body in
his basket swaddled
up in a blanket—
a shroud.

The fire is
chucking out smoke
and we are breathing it
like fire eaters.
We are the freak show
the childless, the mourners.

Our faces are painted
like clowns and the colours
are running down our cheeks.
My lips are glued shut
so I cannot even open
my mouth to comfort her.

A Stranger

He brought me a skull
placed it onto the table
between us
and told
me to hold it.

A stranger so
unrecognisable
unsexed, unfaced,
unborn. A piece
of ivory tilled
from earth.

I felt beneath my hair
for the bones of me
way beneath this thin
layer of flesh and bone
and breath. A feast
one day for a mountain
of crawling maggots sliding

into the crevices of my secrets.
My sockets emptied out,
a prop on an artist's table
illuminated and painted
into the background
of a still life, just fractured
pieces of bone and brush.

Life Drawing

A woman gets tired of painting daisies:
the same wilted vase in varying summers.
I've made it sad and happy
and somewhere in between for the empty

days that roll on like a ladybird
crawling up leaf and leaf and petal.
I ask him to pose, remove his clothes
and let him lie down in the linen and sprawl

for me. Open legs. Gaping mouth. I paint the way
he touches. Lightly then rough then splatter the rest.

An Exchange

I sold him to Charlotte
and helped her hang
his naked body
on the wall of her
bedroom,

his legs open, spread
out on our bed, wrapped
up in the folds of our secrets.

These are the shadows
caught in the curve
of his thighs, his calves,
his feet, unadorned

unpolished man waiting,
hungry, for me to creep
in and move him

but I paint him so still
to keep him there, waiting
for me.

She pays me
more than he's worth
before I leave.

Miniatures

One day I walked into the studio to see him
not stood by a canvas sweeping colour in broad strokes

but hunched over a little table by the window
making tiny brush strokes on a piece of ivory

no bigger than the print of my thumb, a single eye
staring up at us as I leaned over his shoulder while he
created

the faint individual hairs of a blonde eyebrow and dotted
the reflection of the window in her iris. A tiny gaze
destined

to be set into a locket or a tiny pin, stuck into a pocket
and admired in solitary moments, quick peeks

in the corridor or beneath the dining room table,
in the last beams of moonlight. When he finished,

his brush clicked against the table and he leaned back
in his chair, gazing out at the ships bobbing on the murky

waters, letting the paint cure as the lover's eye
watched us, waiting patiently to be delivered.

Pieces of People

As he sat back to admire his work
I wondered what other pieces of people

could be disembodied and singled out,
cast into little mementos in gold trinkets

and snuff boxes, surrounded by pearls and rubies,
cast into jewellery and little picture frames

tucked away for little intimate moments alone,
brushed across their lips. A mouth, a hand, a nipple,

the pink shiny skin of a scar, an ear
to listen while you are away.

As he sips a glass of sherry in the last dregs
of afternoon light, I imagine the pieces of him

I'd keep close and prepare to offer them up,
piecemeal to the highest bidder

Away

I undressed in my room to sit in the solitary
flicker of one candle sputtering
crooked on it candlestick.

I laid in the bed and blew out
the flame, afraid to waste the precious
wax for another time when I may need to
see in the dark.

I wondered if I'd waited and married
another man, when he asked me, if my life
would feel largely the same. If I'd still feel
lonely and sexy and violet and red.

I believe I'd see fewer colours
in my parallel life. I would've never
seen the blue in the ship sails,
the pink of women and men.

That's what I try to see in the darkness—
the blue in the sails like the pools of his eyes
the orange glow of the moon on the choppy waters
as they lick the ships like tongues
whispering.

Keeping Charlotte Company

Some weeks I'd bring my watercolours
and stubs of charcoal to sketch her
as she sipped her tea, capture her leaning
over to grab a slice of cake, the way her lips
opened for bon-bons and petit fours.

I kept them, sometimes look at them
in the studio moonlight in the in between time
between merging my body with his
and the dark blanket of sleep.

Sometimes she paid me for them, folded
them away in a drawer to enjoy in the long depths
of afternoons that stretched out like a cat
in the sun, its claws out, extending.

Selling

I called on the man
with the emerald eyes—alone
on a cold afternoon

my gloves gripping leather
portfolio, climbing
from the carriage

in front of a house rising up
like a crag from the earth
forced upwards shifting plates.

I was shaking in my secret: John thinking
I was elsewhere while we hesitated
over a cup of tea until

he poured me something
stronger and the flush
returned to my cheeks.

My tongue was suddenly a stone
in my mouth. He examined
the work I brought him:

his fingers tracing the charcoal,
pulling the darkness into his fingertips
and blurring the crisp lines

of me and the other women on offer
into something smoother.
He licked his lips and bought
every single portrait I'd offered.

Commission #1

How many studies it took until I was ready to paint her
for the man behind the desk, stacking coins.

I sketched her standing, nude, lying sideways, nude,
from the back with her chemise shifting off her shoulder

and the strong bones of her shoulder blades slicing
through her skin like hungry knives.

I drew her lips a dozen, a hundred times, how her hands
moved in the sheets, how she held on to things: a
  bedpost,
a table edge, the air. I painted the silk ribbons as she
  pulled.

Eventually the misshapen lines of her became blues and
  oranges
the peach juice of her skin, her legs opening up like leaves
  in spring
and in her I found all the shades of pink and green

handing her body to a man who had my own pinned up
  in a secret
room too and in the night when the candles are snuffed
  out, smoke swirling,
we reach for each other through the darkness, our pale
  hands like stars, flickering.

Not a Gentleman

One afternoon I arrived early
and entered Charlotte's room
where her cheeks were flushed

and the air smelled of the mossy
earthy smell of sex, fusty and damp.

I am sorry if I interrupted
you and a gentleman.

Not a gentleman, she said, gesturing
to the window where a woman

in a green gown was tiptoeing down
the long gravel path toward her carriage.

Life is too short to spend it with men,
she said, closing the curtains.

Commission #2

Lucy looked like the night, a full head of dark
midnight curls on top of a face so round and white

she was the moon, shifting the tides, erasing
the shores by tilting her head.

I heard she was good at cards
and fleeced the nobles nightly

was kept by an older man
who could barely move to touch her.

She loosened her chemise but didn't
strip down, played the loose version

of a virgin, smiled at me and told me
what it really took to please a man.

Betty Called on Me

She came on a rainy Monday shivering in the doorway of
the townhouse.
I want to remind you none of this is yours, she said, sipping a cup
of tea.

She sunk her teeth into a piece of cake she was bitter
her husband did not bake. *This is so temporary,* she said.
So I took her to the studio

where I had turned all the portraits of me to the wall. I
showed her
the ones I'd done, the half-completed painting
of a rich man's mistress undressing.

Betty's cheeks flushed with the kind of rosy embarrassment
I've been asked to capture a dozen times, her round
cheeks the full bloom of peony bowing in the sun.

I feel sad for you, she said, surrounded by the grey glow
of rainy studio light, the long shadows cast
over the dozens of paintings of baroque sinfulness.

The silks and velvets, long luxurious fabrics draped
over bodies unabashedly intimate with me. This isn't
something to be ashamed of.

It's a fortune of paint and time, curing
in the studio light. It's the sound
of coins in my own purse.

Pose

Sometimes they asked for pictures of me,
my clothes heaped on the floor. This is my body

in my bed, in their bed, in motion or surprisingly still.
I like the way I look, the way I can make myself look

and disguise my real self with newer colour and paint. But
I have many women now who blush when they undress

in front of me and sometimes I sketch them, their bodies
reduced to swift lines and curls, the curve of a violin, the
suggestion

of a silhouette of a nameless faceless number of a girl
folded up in someone's dresser or hung on the wall.

I have met many men who want to remain anonymous
to have their wants and needs remain behind the lock

and key of their desks, the rooms their wives are kept
from, walls ranged with the torsos of men and women

their arms reaching or covering or touching.
Each one is an ache that goes uncared for, caught

in a moment of time so present and yet past, untouchable
realness worked quickly in studies and bedrooms, quiet

parlours and side rooms full of spare tables and
unpolished
silver. Put them in there, the lovers. Hang them in there,
the lovers. Hide them in there, the lovers.

She Speaks

The winter pressed in, creating
long stretches of darkness
where our portraits turned dim,
candlelit, and often uninspired.

Those days, we wiped our hands
and found a corner in a coffee house
to mingle with the other artists
wasting time between sunlight.

I had learned to speak sometimes,
when I knew the time was right, liberated
by the presence of my patrons, smoking
pipes and looking up from their papers

as I spoke, my words a long curve
like the side of a woman,
up and down and up again.

Commission #3

It was only a portrait of her deep brown eyes,
the front face of a pocket watch for her fiancé

so she sat, rigid, in a hard wooden chair surrounded
by onlooking eyes of the other women we were painting.

The blank pieces of them flashing white
through the colours we'd made.

It only took a day to get her colours right and capture
the way she looked when she spoke about him

a frightened sort of innocence glistening
there in the pale grey light of that rainy Monday

a lusty curiosity, a want. I wanted to capture that want
for her—the lonely longing of waiting for a day

in the distance for the fear of wishing the time away.
She wrung her fingers and tried her best not to

speak to me and when she left the door slammed,
metallic, like coins hitting the ground.

Betty Again

The conversation
of china cups chipping
against their saucers.
I offered to paint her
but she refused.

She doesn't see the beauty
in the secrecy or want to hold
the curve of her body in her hands.
She asks me if I'd sell her
and who else would see.

She didn't want me to see
which parts of hers
were just her own.
She sipped her tea
and I sketched
the palm of her hand
as a promise.

Singular Parts

He poured a second glass
of sherry as I contoured
the pink of nipples:

a miniature for a man
who doesn't want a face
just the disembodied body

parts fixed in tiny frames
pocket-sized breasts
and long fingers clutching
fresh sheets stiff
with sunlight.

I was topless, admiring
the singular parts he'd
requested, admitting

I liked the frozen nature
of capturing my body
in one moment without

the fleeting nature
of the light fading,
the spots on the mirror,
the little flaws that appear
and fade day-to-day.

Just the pink perfection
of brush and light
reflecting off my skin.

Splintered

And suddenly with each portrait he sold
he returned with a new commission for me

until we were duelling in the studio
our half-finished women looking back at us

as we raged at each other, the bitter
coffee in our mouths and the sugar

crystallising between our teeth,
the paint sloughed onto canvas

like raw skin taking a beating, pink and
raw with heat. At the end of the day

he would turn the portraits away and fuck me
hard on the study floor, my knees hammering

the nails into the floorboard
until they splintered.

A Nightmare

An abandoned cottage
in the French countryside
where the sun sets early
and rises earlier
so I am stuck
in perpetually longer and
shorter days that rise
and sink like a chest
crackling with consumption
an unmoving form trapped
in a sick bed, taking
the air and the waters
and the life.

A Conversation

It was a late night
when John had gone
out and Rebecca and I
sat together in the dim
glow of kitchen candlelight,
our lips the burgundy
of our wine. The tea
had been put away.
The silver polished
and stored. The evening
waned into darkness.
We worshiped
the warmth in the hearth.

Have you seen
other women come
through? I asked.
She circled her
fingerprints
on the wine glass.
There have been some.
They've never lasted
as long as you.

My short tenure
under his roof
seemingly a century.
They weren't painters
like you. Pretty faces.
Poets. Courtesans.
Shop girls. Rich daughters

getting more
than a portrait
for their fathers'
sums. A nothingness.

We drink
into the night
and I awaken,
broken, at dawn.

I Drew Betty with Her Clothes on

The rosy hue a face used to looking
into the flames, reaching in to remove
bread, steaming hot in her blistered hands.

He has taught her to fold the dough, white
pillows bubbling up, stretched and rolled and dusted.
They tell each other stories while sprinkling sugar

atop the rolls, crystals shaved off the tall cones, licking
their fingers to dunk in the fallen granules, sweet on the
tongue.

I have seen many bodies clothed and unclothed
but I never know what they will reveal
until the last shift falls and they crawl toward their final
position.

Head up, arms down, no, like that, yes turn your body like
that.
She put the portrait in her pocket, carefully tucked
among her personal items. She hangs the portrait

in a dark corner of their home where she can see it,
inconspicuous
guests unaware of her scandalous sister painting
courtesans in the afternoons, bodies everywhere moving

like that.

Commission #4

How do you want me? Her lips curled
around her words like a vine choking
out the light. She pulled me right in and

melted into the chaise, the buttery velvet
brushing against her bare skin
in our studio, a rare visitor, undressed

in the white sunlight of afternoon
like an afterthought, framed
by the blue sky in the window frame.

She stayed still the full afternoon
as the sun curved around the city, tracing
a map from morning to night

and she stretched her aching body and dressed
slowly, her nimble fingers tonguing
each button hole gingerly until every inch of her

skin was covered again and she left the house.
Onwards toward a long night gripping
the headboard, her clothes ripped off, piled up

on the floor instead of carefully
placed on a chair in the corner of my studio.
When she returned the day after, she only spoke

in sighs and spent her time staring
at the sky and while I wanted her
to look at me, she never even

glanced my way. She tilted her head and
rounded her rosy cheeks like overripe
peaches, so sweet

they were almost rotten.
So I painted her that way:
with her chin tilted toward the sky—

Sit Down

Sit down, Charlotte said pointing
to a chair of bones so brittle they crumbled
under me, the joints creaking like screams.

She had them: the scandal papers
lined up on the table with my name
and my poorly drawn face—aged

and grotesque as a madame
sending her girls to the slaughter.
The whole city suddenly speaking the secret
we'd all promised to keep:

afternoons nude in warm fresh gardens,
the bed chambers flocked and guarded.
The ice slapping into a glass and cracking

in the sun, melting. The women with their clothes
on the floor. And the men, touching
their shoulders with their lips.

Charlotte placed a hand on my knee.
They don't forgive women, she said. *This is the end
for you.* Her voice was like coins emptying to the floor.

Sea Sick

I refused to cry in front of her. I waited for the sweet
seclusion of the crowded street as I navigated my way
home

through the thrashing waves of city footfall. I am sea sick.
Out on the water it was the midnight shade of blue

the knife sharp shimmers of moon thrashing upheaval.
The whole city suddenly sideways. I could become the
ocean and float home.

The rose gold of sunset is an insult. This city
can't look this good when it all falls apart.

His doorstep, the fractures of me. The cold brass in my
hand
for so long it starts to burn so hot I am incinerated,
scattered ash.

I am a light dusting of snowfall. I carry on the whispers of
strangers.
Their shoulders bear me like the heavy edge of a casket.

This is all so temporary. I am so temporary here.
I touch the ridges of the paintings we made. The hips, the
hands.

Hearing my heart in the seashells of my ears while curled
up in bed.
His body against me, breathing, he licks the salt from my
skin.

He pours wine down my throat, heavy and concrete.
I taste the sediment and tannins. We sit in the dark

bottom of an amber bottle and count the flickers
and sputters from the candles.

We hold ourselves there in the darkness: what's outside?
There's a storm surging. It might just wash us away.

The Fall

In the morning, we ache.
We heave within the belly
of a ship. We watch the sun
curl across the sky.

From the soft spaces
in the studio, our limbs
woven together.
Where he ends,
I begin. Where I end,
he is there again.

We are surrounded
by the unfinished bodies
of our commissions.
Their incomplete
torsos and missing
limbs, white space
waiting to be filled in

like a forgotten city of gold
shimmering under the surface
of the sea. I can see

the letters on the table,
the news we already know:
the purse strings are drawn.

We are the fallen tulips
in the still life.
We are the petals
crunching under your shoe.

Reunion

It was mid-afternoon on a street in Paris
when I saw her, relaxed in the cafe wicker
beside a man smoking a cigarette, breathing
it into the air like a bored cloud.

A long lazy afternoon for them.
She scraped the last bits of cream
from her bowl and licked the spoon clean.

She called out for John—she knew his name.
Her swish, her hands suddenly on him, on me,
les bisous. An introduction. My name on her lips
still wet with cream. She introduces her lover.

She asks where we're staying and where we're going.
She mention her travels, her paintings,
her exhibitions, her independence.

She sits back down before I can even speak
and we shuffle to another street. John's body
against mine, clutching.

What He Says About Her

She had talent but no skill, a waste
flitted away on watercolour portraits
of babies and florals—a made up garden
blooming wildly inside her empty head.

She could not hold the brush the way you can,
see the colour so vibrantly. Your strokes
are longer and faster, they make her look
like an amateur. Between you and I,

you are the artist.

Notorious

John had gone to visit a former patron that afternoon
while I sipped coffee and sketched passersby
at a cafe near the river, shielding my face

from the shimmering sun and the prying eyes
of those who'd heard about me
and my shameful sinful art.

Elizabeth? A voice rose above the clatter
of cup and chatter and carts on the cobblestone.
A man was waving from across the street.

I hid my face from him with the brim of my hat.
He crossed the busy street and sat beside me
like me knew me, smelling of fresh linen and florals,

his cheeks flushed with sun and the slightest hint
of sweat on his brow. *Mademoiselle, is it really you?*
The notorious Elizabeth Miller?

I put my sketching pad on the table to look at him,
grinning at me over my empty cup. Why do you ask?

Pierre

Pierre was an eccentric, a hat maker by trade
who told me mine was rather ugly,
how he'd make me a new one,

and ordered a coffee, which I paid for,
then asked me to paint him.

Without a proper studio? I started.
I'm not painting those portraits anymore, I continued
a waterfall of excuses gushing from me—none accepted.

It is good money, he said. *And who would turn down
a chance to be painted by the most notorious artist in Europe?*

A Portrait for Lovers

When John returned home, he found a naked man in our bed,
glancing over his shoulder like Venus, waiting on a lover.

It was for a lover, he said, a man he loved who loved him in secret.
A small gift for him, he said. And as I painted him, my hands traveled
back to the museum where the sculptures sat, waiting for their lovers too.

What in the devil is this? John threw his sketchbook
across the room and the pages settled to the floor like snow.
This is Pierre. I stumbled. He asked me to paint him.

You are a ruined woman! There is no painting him!
There is no painting anyone now or ever. You are a still life artist.
You paint flowers and goblets and fucking fruit.

Pierre slid from the sheets and began dressing. I was almost done
with the sketch, enough to finish without him
but I knew the details would be off—

was the freckle on his right shoulder or left?
Did I paint all the shadows on his vertebrae right?
He left, wordlessly, as John hung his head

and asked, *Do you ever want me to work again?*

Invitation

When the letter arrived it smelled like her. Somehow
the sea, the waxy scent of her coloured lips, the green
of late spring. An invitation with my name on it, alone,

with a space on the wall for me and my name, my body—
the short and long strokes of it—on its own, breathing
and untouchable, bathing in the spotlight of their eyes

while they wondered if what I've drawn is really
  underneath
the weight of this dress—and isn't that the real secret—
if it's real or just drawn up from fiction, these twists and
  curves.

I just like that she remembered my name.

Delivery

I finished the painting while John was out
on long afternoons courting patrons, seeking work—
honest work without secrecy and stigma.

Pierre looked like a God—a body
awaiting a lover, his skin glowing,
thrust forth from the background.

I wrapped it carefully in brown paper to deliver
and met him at his apartment, a decadent property
filled with jewel toned velvets and feathers

and air filled with fined dust particles
that filtered the light like snow but never settled.

He made us coffee and offered a plate of cakes
that we slowly devoured as the afternoon passed,
admiring the unshrouded work I'd done for him:

a male masterpiece, at once beautiful and masculine,
his lines softened and sharpened when they should be.

The English really know how to ruin a good time, he said.
Who could destroy someone as talented as you?

He kissed my cheek and sent me back to a dark apartment
where I waited all night for John to return.

The Exhibition

She'd painted a platter of oysters, their slimy flesh
dripping
in lemon juice, the peel curled up on the side, a snake.

She gave me a glass of champagne that dotted my tongue
with a spell so I could not speak. I saw some of your
portraits.

More interesting than this cup of wine, she said, eyeing
my still life, some wine, some bread, some clutching at
straws.

She held my hand. She stole more champagne.
She whisked me through the crowds

to a powder room where we sealed out the baritone
murmur of men and stood, alone, in the candlelight.

She kissed the curl of my neck as I watched us
in the looking glass: a couple of apparitions, shining.

She held the curve of my waist and sipped her
champagne.
Don't marry him, she said. *You're a better painter than that.*

That Night

he didn't curl his body around me, the sweet smell
of the tobacco on his skin, his fingers curled into my hair.

He slipped into sleep without a word, a finger
on my lips, without telling me the colour

of the day and whether it was a cerulean blue
or chartreuse, the faint beige of a taxidermy beast
looking out at us with shiny amber eyes.

The sun rose to greet my sleeplessness
and I made us coffee that we drank in a long dark silence,

draining the cups to the fine grains
at the bottom, our tongues bitter and black.

Saying Goodbye to Marie

I met her in town
the day before we left Paris.

We ordered coffees and cakes
and lazed in the shade of the cafe terrace,

gossiping about a man
who thought he had a chance with her,

a lover who'd left her scorned,
and the Italian she traveled with,

at once very beautiful but spoke little
and didn't want anything but to touch her,
which she doesn't seem to mind.

It's only an hour from the city.
You will visit, no? she said,

brushing the sweet crust
of sugar from my lips.

The Summer Home

We left Paris for a space we could be together
in the long peach flavoured nights of summer.

The long grass brushed our legs. The air: floral
and hot with lavender blooming in the fields.

The earth hummed with bees, a murmur that muted
the dull dirge of the city we'd brought with us.

A yellow cottage. A garden. A bedroom
for two. A studio we could melt into and build

up the heavy layers of paint, strip off
our clothes, and swim naked in the stream.

He undressed me in the field
when we got there, my fingers brushing

the seeds from their pods and scattering
them, dry and hot, while he painted me.

Summer Settling

His red hair was the sun in the long
blue sky of summer that stretched before us:

walking through the tall grasses brushing
our legs like whispering fronds

and while I bathed in the stream he sat on the edge
sketching the splashes against my skin.

We settled into our near solitude like a long stretch
of sky or stream or sinew struggling in a long held pose

shaking tensely as we moved our bodies to fit a mould,
twisting and turning and feeling the sweat on our skin,

humid and sticky from the sun, pink-scorched and
  freckled
so my teeth looked lead white in the daylight

shimmering ripples in the water
so cool against my soul.

The Studio

We began to fill the walls with the long strokes of us—
bodies, wine coloured, streaked with the bracken moss

of forest floor, the murk of river, the white sails
I used to dream of, weather-worn and sun bleached.

I can see all my flaws, dented hips, the round of my
stomach,
maligned brush strokes carelessly laid and overlooked, left
to set

forever. The smell of turpentine, time dissolved
into the rainbow of a bucket swirling with the day's
labour

melting away. He shows me how to rinse them clean.

The Maid

He hired a maid that spoke nothing
but French and slipped in and out
of the house like a ghost

so the only traces of her
were the objects she shifted,
the new loaf of bread in the kitchen,

the dishes cleaned and drying
in the sink, the linens sunning
themselves on the line. Some days

she would linger, humming her hymns
in the studio, pausing with her hands
on the bowls of fruit we'd planned to paint,

shiny and perfect before they succumbed
to the heat, but then it was back to the washing
lines, the dusting, the dishes in the sink.

Sometimes she erased her footsteps
on the way out like she'd never arrived
and never left. It was just me, waiting
for the sun to rise and sink and fall and arrive.

Scrubbed Clean

It felt like I could breath here in the lavender scented air
full of bees swirling from one blossom to the next.

My lungs cleared out the last of London left
in me, the thick layer of dirt and soot swept into me,

kicked up from the streets, coating the whole town
in dinge and grime. The windows streaked with rain,

shifting the grit like a slime, watching it cascade down
in those bitter cold rainy days, sat round the sputtering fire.

A yellow cottage caked in florals, a whole summer
to bask in the colours, unmuddled and pure pigment.

Away from the dark caverns of terrace house, where
we had to climb and climb to find the one room in the city

with real light, his windows scrubbed clean.
I rinsed my hand in the stream and breathed.

Hand Prints

In the sunlight,
I can see
the marks
from my hands
where he pressed
me and I'd held on.

I want to paint
them, the ghosts
of our desires,
transparent like
jellyfish floating—

thin clouds whispering
across the sky. His breath
on my neck as I prepare
the canvas. I steady
myself on the table. I mix
the right colours.

Why do you still draw me?

To memorise the lines of your face, the way
your cheekbones hollow, the curve
of your jaw, the dented scar on your chin.

It is to remember, to mark the time.
There was the day I noticed the line
where your smile creases your cheek
and I draw it darker on darker days.

I can capture the sunlight in your eyes,
the blue glow of cloud, the shadow of snow,
how you change with the seasons.

Skin. Body. Shape. You making breakfast.
You drinking your tea. You taking off
my dress. You looking at me.

Night Garden

In the middle of the night, I sometimes wake
and wander into the garden to see what colours
the night paints it. I bathe in the silver moon glow
and count the stars. We are so utterly alone
here. I hear nothing. I rip at the velvet leaves and rub
them between my palms to perfume my skin.
I like to feel and smell the earthy green when I think.
Plant tendrils curled into the stones to pull the old walls down.
The gate creaked. The moon swallowed me whole.

A Little Death

He took the carriage into town alone
and came back long after the sky hung
heavy with night. He smelled of tobacco
and fortified wine, his lips, red
and sweet, seemed licked clean.

I wanted to wipe him from this canvas
like a misplaced tree, a malformed cat
arching its back but he clung to me

in the bed, wrung his hands through my hair
and twisted his limbs with mine until
where did my body begin and his end—inside me

and screaming—and charcoal smudges and yellow
sparks like flickering wicks—glowing—erupting.
Midnight mass. A funeral. A little death
shaking the shivers from my skin.

The Monotony of Our Summer

I begin to measure out our lives
in empty tubes. The curled ends
of paint reaching toward the tendrils
of sun streaming through the window.

The minutes ticking
by in the swish of brush stokes
like sand in an upturned hourglass
pouring away our time.

The Pietà

One night we walked the mile
into town and drank wine
with strangers. He spoke
broken French and I listened
with deaf ears to the song
of a new language.

We made love in a field
on the way home
and as he pushed into me
I tilled the still-warm soil
with my fingers and wrapped
the night air around us
like a blanket.

The next morning he painted
the picture that would make him famous:
my body, draped in blue, as I posed
still aching, going golden in the summer
sun. My dry lips still purple with wine
and cracking.

Dreaming

Some nights I go to bed
early and think
let me into my dreams.

I dream
in big blossoms
of colour like paint
splattered on the floor
blood drops, rains drops
painting the bricks
and the pavements
grey.

The big silken petals
of poppies lifted
in the wind and drifting
like wounded butterflies.
The spilt goblet of wine.

The crash. An upturned table.
The sound of a heave
at the door. A man
breathing wine
into my face,
his beard dripping.

He sleeps.
I sleep,
empty.

The Bathers

One afternoon I wandered down to the creek with some loose papers
and a fresh piece of charcoal to sketch the fresh tendrils of new leaves
stretching toward the sun and stumbled on two women bathing,

their clothes heaped on the riverbank and white breasts like moons
in the sunlight, laughing splashing and soaking each other with the new summer
air thick with pollen, the yellow dust of petal centre and tree leaf
gathered up and sprinkled like fairy dust from the overflowing legs of bees.

They did not see me, crouched down in the greenery, tracing their bodies, twisting
and swimming though the water, arms wrapping around each other throwing,
pushing until their fingers and toes are creased and wrinkled like peach pits
gripping the surface of the earth and climbing out
to drip dry in the sun so golden and freckled and trembling.

Sleeplessness

In the hollow belly of darkness,
a new moon night shrouded
the cottage in black silk
as I lay in the empty bed like a tomb.

His space waiting to be filled,
just an indentation in the mattress
where he used to lay beside me.

The crickets warmed their strings
and bowed a long incoherent symphony
that filled the long silence

as I dug the paint from my nails,
counting the seconds ticking by
from the clock in the hall long
into the empty night.

Heartache

I waited three days in loneliness before I left,
caught a carriage back to Paris for the night
and arrived at Pierre's door with a prayer

he would be there and he was. He held me
in the doorway of his apartment before pulling me in
and pouring two glasses of wine, clinked joylessly

in the dying sunlight. He did my hair. He took me
to a bar filled with dancing men dressed in velvet
touching and kissing each other in public and we drank

until the room spun around us, until we used each other
as a crutch to walk home down the riverside
and through the streets to his door.

I woke up beside him with my head throbbing,
eying the portrait I'd done of him, still hung
tentatively in the corner, ungifted.

Assumptions

Over breakfast,
he begged me
to stay.

The heat
in the city
was already
oppressive

and I feared
John's reaction
if he returned
and found me
missing—

the assumptions
he'd make
about the woman
he'd ruined.

I heaved
through the long
rutted journey
back to home
and found it
still there, empty.

The Landscape

He returned that evening, filthy,
practically bleeding wine.
He smelled like shame
as if we had any left.

He fell into bed
and slept through the night
to late morning

when I was poised in the garden,
working on a version of a landscape,
dying to add the silhouette

of Marie to the scene
but as he looked over my shoulder,
it was pastoral.

He grunted
and wandered
back inside alone.

Summer

It was the most alone I'd been since we'd met:
those days when he did not return I spent wondering
what body he was drawing and what wine warmed his lips,
what made him leave and what made him stay away.

I took off my clothes and stood in the garden. I met my
reflection
in the window blurred out like the airbrushed goddesses
in our elicit paintings, their wide brush strokes and slender
expressions, a rosy type of seduction.

I painted my body in the bright of midday sun
against the daisies pushing out of dirt, against the buzz
of bees in the beds. I breathed the thick sweltering air
and glistened in the window while I waited and painted

the best art I'd done—those blooming bouquets of
summer,
my thighs aching, my clothes blowing on the line after a
swim.

Ache

I started to enjoy the long nights alone
draped in the silk of midnight moonlight

smelling the jasmine petals still warm
with afternoon sun. It's an edible moon

something soft to dip my tongue into
to chase with the last sandy dregs

of wine, my lips stained purple
and my feet gone black in the dirt.

I touched my toes to the sky
and prayed for her and some God
somehow whispered back.

A Visitor

I got a letter from her
on one of those long
humid afternoons.

John had left
the night before
and I'd spent

the time sweating
and pacing the garden
in my bare feet,

snapping the sun
scorched plants
in my fingers.

She wanted to buy
the painting I'd shown the night
she stole the champagne

and kissed me.
She was stopping
by that afternoon.

She was already rolling
down the dusty road
toward me.

Rosebud

She stood in front of the painting
and touched her fingers
to the table top, little tents
filled with fire.

She smelled like lavender fields.
She glowed. She paid me
or the painting
that I wasn't proud of
and asked to see the others.

I led her to the studio
where she sighed
over still life after still life,
dark and brooding.
The closed buds
just before they bloom,
the droplets on the table top.

She wanted them all
but said I was wasted
on paintings of flowers
and rosebuds.

Breathing

Marie started visiting the yellow cottage
with teacakes and we'd sit in the field licking
the melting sugar from our fingers.

I drew her gathering bouquets of flowers
and bringing them into the house. I drew her placing
them in the tall vases until the whole house was a garden.

She'd had the kind of education
that teaches you to arrange flowers and marry rich
and bring teacakes to an afternoon visit.

In the heat, we'd strip down to the thin
of frilly chemise, unlaced the bodices
of corset and bone and let our bodies breathe.

Strangers

He painted empty places in my portraits—a hole
where my left hip used to be, a dip where I used to
round out, a space in my chest, hollow and empty
to the sky, the meadow flowers, the vase in the window.

Invisible pieces of myself, replaced with backdrop, with
the body parts of other women. These are not my hands,
my back, my breasts, my nose. My body transformed
into unrecognisable women: sallow and jagged bone.

The uninviting lips of strangers hang in the studio
with me so I can watch them become me as I paint
a broken vase, its blooms browned and burnt.

until I am looking at her
face, peach and porcelain
rising above me, fucking me
like a summer moon.

When did she become him
become me? These portraits
are both of us, carved up.
The best pieces, divided
into body parts, a reconstructed
monster, shaped like a woman
re-birthed in pastel.

The discarded pieces of us
left in the wide brush strokes
of the dark background
close enough I could reach in
and grab them: a grave robbed
skull, smooth and dead in my hand.

Another Still Life

The clock wound down the hours until its hands
dissolved like sugar on my tongue.

We pulled all the silver out
of the drawers and our sacred hiding places

and set it all out in jagged rows
the china stacked up, uneven and dangerous.

Our paints our hands our canvases
until our fingers are a sunset

and we compared our images,
our bodies, the long brush stroke curve

of the plates, the sky, the tiles around the fire
the paint stacked up—reaching out for us

built up around the edges
of the cutlery, the chalices, the candelabra

the wine glasses poured generously
a thick blanket pulled around us: the softness

her curves her peaks and troughs. Her afternoons
her mornings. Her green ribbons. Her goodbyes

when the clock chimes again.
Her sunburnt cheeks—still blushing.

A Portrait of Marie

I paint her as I see her, just before she takes off her clothes
for me. Pleading eyes like rock pools, drying up in the sun.

I dip my brush in, create colour, let the paint melt and drip
sticky sweet down my hands. When she undresses,

it is an act, her arms folding and unfolding like feathered fans.
Her dress is a heap on the floor and instead of the seams, she is
seamless,

unstitched, pink and ruinous. I can feel the texture of her skin
shivers—the weave of canvas. I can hear the rattle of her chest

when she breathes.

I Filled the Yellow Walls with Pictures of Her

With long lengths of canvas and her gauzy summer
dresses,
the long pink ribbons that lace and open her up, back
bones
protruding from her arched spine leaning in to grab a
handful
of daisies. The polka dots of petals on the grass.

They lined the studio like vases of tulips and zinnias, the
long fingers
of lilies reaching. I hide them behind the bowls of grapes
and strawberries
I painted still lifes on the days she wasn't around: the cakes
she left behind cut up
and crumbling, empty bottles he had left behind like an
archaeological dig

discovering the man who used to live here. I don't know
where he is
or where he belongs. When I hear him stumbling on the
gravel on the way home
I place the mirrors back in the hallway and hide her body
behind mine as the candles flicker.

The clock in the hall clicks and machines its way through
time. I let him
climb on top of me and grip the sheets. I count the stars
outside the window, knock
the glass from the side table and cut my hand open, suck
the wound,
sour like a lemon, until my mouth runs dry.

Ash

He found us one afternoon in the tall summer grass
our chemises pulls down to our waists, our breasts
tracking
the sun like daisies. She was reading aloud in French.

I could not understand a word but I liked
the way she held her mouth when she spoke: her lips
wider but smaller, her tongue closer to her teeth.

He stood on the crest of the hill that hid the house from
us
watched me bite into a strawberry and stain my lips
then he disappeared before she even knew he was there.

Inside, he put a knife through my painting of her. She
smoked
a bone pipe and puffed out little clouds of carelessness
into the empty sky while inside he disintegrated.

Summer Wine

When she kissed me goodbye, her lips
tasted like the hot salt of summer sticky bodies
in the sun, the wisps of our hair stuck down to our skin.

I found him, purple mouthed, smoking a pipe by the door
the green glass of bottle catching the last dregs of sunlight
as the sky turned Chardonnay turned Cabernet
  Sauvignon turned

the deep colour of fresh bruises blooming up to the
  surface
like tea leaves unfurling in the pot. I put myself in his
  arms
and pressed the heat of me against him, his skin pricked

with the hum of summer wine drunk and he smelled like
  sweat
and smoke and sandalwood. I leaned in and licked the
  salt
from the skin of his neck, feeling my teeth press.

I could have punctured him like the portrait
lying in tatters inside: the long bandages
of a burial, a funeral, a shroud.

with the care of curator
or a nurse mending war wounds.

The cotton swabs soaking
up the rust red of insides.

I now understand the bodies
   of man and woman, how they come

together, the symmetry and asymmetry
of breast and buttock and bone, arches

and long lines, the geometry of face and back,
the residue you leave behind, your palm.

I mix the colours of your body.
I make them move, appreciate

the long and short of it. I fall in love
with the picture of you

the act of creating and
recreating you.

A Letter from Betty

A letter from Betty arrived one afternoon
as I was painting a portrait of myself,
staring at my body in the long dappled
glass of the hallway mirror.

I unfolded it and smeared vermillion
on the page from my fingertips.
She'd had a baby boy in the deep
hours of night. She told me

when it's late and she rises to feed him,
she sits in a chair beside the portrait
I'd made of her and as she rocks her baby
boy in her arms and while he feeds
she stares at the body that used to be hers.

She tells me what it feels like to be torn
right open from the bottom up, the magic
of birth and blood, how pink and red
it all was, the sound of screaming

into the darkness of night and blacking out.
It was a terrible miracle, she said.
She was so very tired.
He was so very beautiful.

The Last Supper

That night he came home and lit the cottage on fire
with candlelight until the whole place glowed
and our skin, pink with heat, glistened in the flickering
glow.

The candle wax pooled on the table
and our portraits watched us eat
in the silence of countryside symphony,

the sunlight faded away to nothing,
the heat of the day whisked away in a swirl
of moonlight, red wine hot on our tongues

like hate. Is this hate? Is this what it means
to hate? We cleaned our plates and wiped up the juices
with the last of our bread.

We sat outside in the garden, throwing
our empty bottles into the tall grass until
we were too stupid to move.

I emptied my stomach into the gutter.
I let him hold me when I screamed
at him for leaving. I let him restrain me

when I went to ruin all the work we'd done.
His hands on my wrists and his lips grazing
my hips. Everything was the colour blood red.

I opened my mouth and swallowed
the whole evening whole. I pulled the air
right out and let the smoke curl
as I extinguished the flame.

Blank

In the morning,
he left again.

He left me naked
in his bed

staring
at a blank canvas.

The Invitation

A picnic laid out on a blanket in the tall grass
with purple and yellow flowers bending
in the breeze, scattering their fertile seeds.

I'm going back to Italy. A show in Florence,
a new place to create and display her art.
She is following her lover home

to a house somewhere in the countryside,
like here but hotter. She licked the cream
from inside of a pastry she'd brought

while I churned the emptiness
in my stomach to a spiralling nausea.

She bit into a strawberry and it bled
down her chin, reddened her lips.
The seeds stuck between her teeth.

I want you to come with me. We can show
the whole world your art.

And when she touched the side of my face,
I felt the sugar on her fingertips tearing through me,
jagged and rough.

These Are the Bodies I Know

I didn't know there were choices before her:
bent over her sketchbook, her palms grey
from the charcoal gripped tightly in her hands.

Her fingers were dancers working their way from one end
of the stage to the next, flowing in the late morning
light cascading through the gallery.

The academies and courses she was denied,
the endless pages of men she carved up
with her charcoal, creating their crests and falls

their shadows and lightness where their bodies
crease and fold and harden. Her hands tracing their
  outlines.

My body, her face moving toward my lips still stinging
with champagne, her paintings, the oysters, the pearls.

Don't marry him, she said. *Come with me,* she also said.
I felt the warmth of her lover's hand still on her waist. It
  wasn't a life
for me to become a ghost following behind her.

It was all about her until it suddenly wasn't
and I painted her for the last time, her straps falling
from her shoulders in the parlour, capturing the sugar
on her lips shining sweetly: the long lost mouth of a lover.

I owe her every body I paint. These are the bodies *I*
  know.
She's all of them. I can see the reflection of her in their
  eyes.

Heat

The day she left, I followed her
to meet the carriage.

She took the canvas from my hands,
a portrait of her body in all the shades

of pinks and greens she wore on her skin
in the garden at the yellow cottage.

She kissed the palm of my hand,
a hummingbird hovering in cardiac distress,

then climbed aboard. The coach pulled away
into the rutted road worn dry in the summer sun

like the ground could crack right open and eat me:
a teacake melting on the earth's tongue.

Without

For days, I laid around the cottage
walking through the rooms like a ghost
feeling the emptiness of the space,
hollow like a grave before the funeral,

a gaping hole waiting to be filled.
John had gone, his easel left barren,
a blank canvas left untouched and unwanted
with no promise of return.

On a cloud covered afternoon,
I sat outside and painted the garden,
the lavender petals dried on the plants,
the whole world turned a silver gray.

The air hung thick and humid,
sticking strands of hair to my skin.
This was what was left:
a hollow belly, a dark cavernous den.

The maid flitted in and out,
barely acknowledging me.
I am a spectre, foreign
and transparent, fading.

A Letter from Charlotte

After a long week of loneliness
a letter from Charlotte arrived
with an invitation to return.

The news had scattered like ash
on the beaches, washed away in the tides
of gossip that swelled and swept
others out to sea with them.

I was nearly forgotten,
a perfect reason to return
and start again.

That night, I dreamt of the sound
of coins in my pocket.
There was a naked woman

plucking an apple from a branch
and tearing its flesh with her teeth.
There was a long journey ahead.

Amends

I wrote a letter to my mother
that swirled like the tendrils of vines reaching

long petals, blooming ink spreading
out in the spaces between fibre and fear.

Everything is an ink blot, this whole letter
and life. I told her about Paris.

I told her about the moon and the way, recently,
I have begun to paint flowers again. I leave out

the details of Marie's hands arranging the long stems
in the vases, the women in the paintings I've made, peachy
rose

and softened curve, their long bodies like instruments—
the hum of the orchestra warming up beneath the stage.

I don't mention the way my lips were wine-stained,
flattened out, how my nose freckled, my shoulders sun-
goldened,

my clothes looser, unbuttoned, unworn. My lovers,
my love, the slosh of paint on the board.

The Return

The day I left, he still hadn't come home. I'd spent the night
and day packing my canvases to journey back home.

Perhaps he realised he had nothing more to teach me
because I surely had so much more to learn.

As I watched the yellow cottage melt into horizon,
I thought of all the landscapes I hadn't painted there:

all the hills I had seen and yet they so suddenly escaped me.
I thought of the houses I'd left and the houses that could've been.

I thought of the ships lulling down the river, its brown water lapping
at the shore. I thought of the parting of lips, the way he held

his paint brushes between his fingers, the colours that we'd made.
I wondered how long it would be until he noticed I'm gone

and wondered where exactly I was going. A whole world of portraits
and windows to look out of. It was all so temporary.

I touched the keys in my pocket like brass bones, a chiming clock
telling the hour. I pictured the ghosts of familiar furniture, white sheets

to fold away in his terrace house as I rock down the road,
pitch and sway
across the channel, and as, out of the fog, London
appeared

in the gray distance, I sketched the skyline
to the edge of the page but it just kept going.

More Books by Amy Ellis

He is the Monster
Fault
Modern Ghost

About the Author

Amy Ellis lives in London and works in publishing. She has a BA in Creative Writing from Longwood University and a Masters in Digital Publishing from Oxford Brookes University. She enjoys writing poems, knitting, gardening, and playing with her dog.

Find her online at amy-ellis.com or on social media @amesplaza.

Printed in Great Britain
by Amazon

81246429R00098